OWEN THE OCTOPUS

TRIES TO FLY

Written and Illustrated by
Tami Boyce

ISBN: 0692785116
ISBN-13: 978-0692785119

Tami Boyce Design
Charleston, South Carolina

To Alexandra, Joey, and Griffin.
I hope you never stop trying to fly.

At first glance, Owen seemed like a typical octopus. He had eight tentacles. He was a great swimmer and was also very flexible.

Most octopuses were happy swimming in the ocean, but Owen wanted more. He had lots of dreams—**BIG** dreams—but his favorite daydream was when he imagined he could fly.

Owen would spend most of his days watching the animals that lived above the water. He wondered what it was like to soar through the clouds, feeling the wind and sunlight all around. One day, he decided to try to make this dream come true.

The other octopuses laughed when Owen told them about his plan to fly, but Owen remained focused. He would not let their laughter make him give up on his dream. "Octopus or not, I'm going to put these tentacles to work and become the most amazing flying machine anyone has ever seen!"

Owen was a very hard worker. He spent all of his time reading and researching, knowing that there must be some way to make his eight-legged body fly.

He read piles of books about inventors and adventurers who accomplished their dreams when no one thought they could.

After all of his research, Owen knew exactly what to do. "I'm going to make a catapult!"

Owen got right to work. "I wonder why no one has tried this before," he thought. "Once I'm in the air, the wind should take care of the rest!"

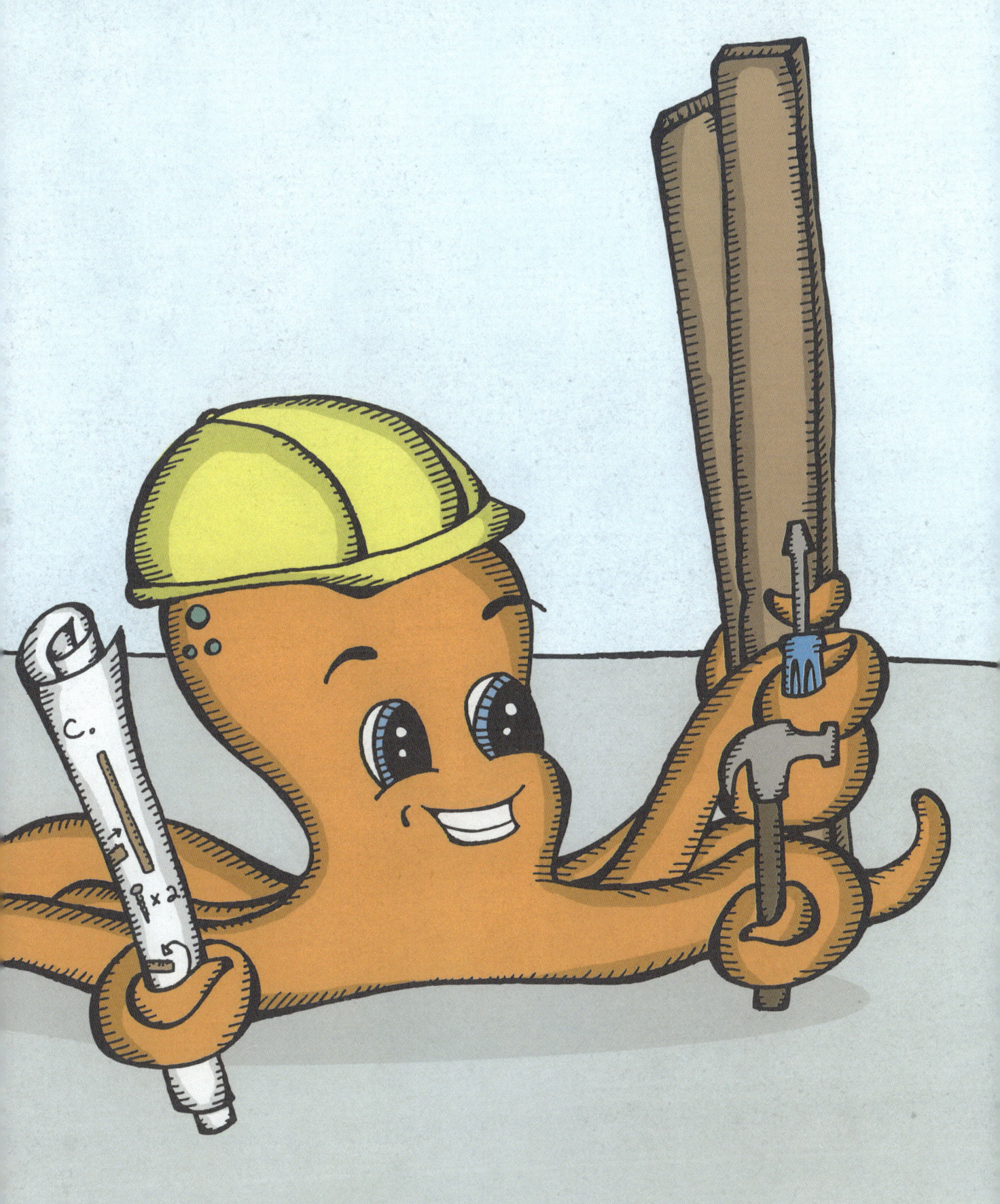

With dedication and hard work, Owen's catapult was finally ready. He strapped himself into the bucket, ready to launch himself into his first flight!

The next thing he knew, Owen was flying!
He was finally a soaring, majestic creature!
Owen was on top of the world...

... for five seconds.

Unfortunately, Owen's plan didn't take gravity into account. After the brief flight, he was slapped flat against the ocean surface at a very fast speed.

Although Owen was pretty
banged up, his dream was not
hurt at all. "I can't let ONE little setback discourage
me," said Owen. "Perhaps I don't need a fancy
invention at all—I just need wings!
Birds fly with only two, but I could
use eight wings to make me
fly higher and faster!"

Owen spent days collecting feathers to build his wings. With much excitement, he was now ready to complete the new additions for his tentacles.

He strapped on the wings
and headed for the surface.
He couldn't wait to taste the freedom of flight!
He pulled himself up onto a buoy
and reached for the sky!

Owen began flapping…and flapping…but for some reason, the wings didn't lift him into flight as he expected. He flapped faster and faster…and harder and harder, but Owen still didn't fly. It seemed the only thing these wings were good for was making a wet, splashy mess.

Once again, Owen felt disappointed but not defeated. He knew he just had to put the *right* plan into action, so he tried other ideas.

There was a failed rocket…

a balloon

mishap…

and an

ineffective

superhero cape.

Eventually, Owen started to doubt himself.
"Perhaps everyone is right. I'm just an octopus.
I should stick to what I'm good at and
give up my dream," he said.

Owen was then greeted by a flock of his bird friends, who asked him what was wrong. He described his dream as well as his attempts and failures. He admitted he was ready to give up. "Octopuses just can't fly," Owen told the birds.

One of the birds then said to Owen, "Why didn't you ask us? We can work together to help you achieve your dream. Count on us, and before you know it, you'll be soaring in the clouds!"

And with the help of the birds, Owen took flight! He couldn't believe it! The wind rushed past his face, and the sunlight surrounded him. He was so grateful for this perfect moment.

They flew and flew until Owen was ready to land.

Owen was the happiest he had ever been! And in that instant, he realized something very important. Sometimes, especially when your dream is bigger than you are, you just need a little help from your friends to accomplish it.

Friends **CAN** help octopuses fly! Maybe now it's Owen's chance to turn the birds into Olympic swimmers!

THE END

A Note from the Author/Illustrator

"There is freedom waiting for you,
On the breezes of the sky,
And you ask "What if I fall?"
Oh but my darling,
What if you fly?"

— Erin Hanson

I've been told before that I have a "childlike" way of looking at the world, and I take this as a very high compliment. Young children possess a wide-eyed view of the world—a sweet, unfiltered view that isn't jaundiced by self-doubt or cynicism.

Somewhere along the way, many of us find ourselves talked out of our dreams by naysayers. I hope Owen's story helps your children dare to dream big and to keep trying no matter the odds. I also wish for everyone that, through the beauty of failure, you not only continue to challenge yourself but also learn that it's okay to lean on others. Ask for help when you need it, and your friends will come through. Mine do. And so will yours.

Tami Boyce is a Charleston-based illustrator and graphic designer. "Owen the Octopus" is her first children's book. To see more of her work, please visit tamiboyce.com

65927027R00024

Made in the USA
Charleston, SC
07 January 2017